Peter Millett was born in New Zealand. He
was first published aged nine when one of his
humorous poems appeared in the national press.
He has since gone on to publish a great many
children's books in New Zealand, including picture
books and educational books. He has a passion for
zany English humour and Spike Milligan is one
of his all-time heroes. He lives with his family in
Auckland.

# BOY ZERO
## WANNABE HERO

# THE PETRIFYING PLOT OF THE PLUMMETING PANTS

Peter Millett

Illustrations by Steve May

**ff**

*faber and faber*

FOR GEOFFREY AND GEORGIA

First published in 2010 by
Faber and Faber Limited
Bloomsbury House, 74–77 Great Russell Street,
London, WC1B 3DA

Typeset by Faber and Faber
Printed in England by CPI BookMarque, Croydon

A CIP record for this book
is available from the British Library

ISBN 978–0–571–25247–3

2 4 6 8 10 9 7 5 3 1

# CONTENTS

# SUPERHERO OR SUPERZERO?

Charlie Applejack was sitting on his bed reading his favourite book of all time: *Commander Ron: My Life as an Extremely Cool Superhero and Other Stories To Make You Go Wow*. He was nose deep in the middle of Commander Ron's most thrilling adventure, 'The Day it Rained Killer Zombie Iguanas', when suddenly he heard his mother calling from downstairs in the lounge.

'Charlie, Charlie – the post has arrived.'

Charlie snapped Commander Ron's book shut and rocketed down the stairs.

1

'I'll get it!'

He hurtled through the front door and down the path to the box by the gate with his arms flapping like an out-of-control bumble bee. Dad waved at him furiously. 'Charlie, watch out for the . . .'

**KERRUNCH**

' . . . post box!'

Charlie brushed the shattered remains of the box off his sweatshirt.

'Oops. Sorry, Dad. I did it again. Sometimes I just don't know my own strength.'

Dad picked up the pieces of broken wood off the grass.

'Son, you gotta slow down. That's the third box you've destroyed already this week. I don't have any more left. Now, I know you're really excited about the news you're expecting from the Super School, but . . .'

Charlie suddenly noticed a small white object wedged in the middle of a bed of petunias.

'Dad, Dad, look it's here.' He reached down and picked up a mud-stained envelope. 'It's my letter

from the Super School.'

Dad held the letter up in the air.

'So it is.'

Charlie, Mum, Dad, and Charlie's sister Trixie sat around the kitchen table eagerly eyeing up the crumpled envelope. Trixie thrust out her hand and grabbed it.

'Dad said I could open it first,' she cried.

Dad plucked the envelope out of Trixie's hands.

'No, I didn't.' He passed it over to Charlie. 'This is Charlie's letter. He's been expecting it all year.'

Charlie ran his finger along the top of the

envelope. He passed it over to Mum. 'I can't open it. I'm too nervous. You do it.'

'Are you sure, dear?'

'Yep.'

Mum carefully peeled open the seal and looked inside. 'It's a letter from Alfred Heath, the director of the Super School. Do you want me to read it out loud?'

Charlie nodded.

'Dear Master Applejack, thank you for your recent application to join our world-famous superhero training school. We were thrilled to receive your application, and we were also impressed with the positive attitude you displayed during your superpowers testing exams.'

Charlie beamed.

'However, after reviewing your test results, we feel that your superpowers are simply not super enough to meet the high standards of our school. Sadly, we cannot offer you a position on our superhero training programme. We wish you all the best for your future, and hope that you have a super day.'

Charlie's jaw dropped. Dad looked at Mum.
Mum looked down at her hands. Trixie yawned
and started picking her nose.

'What? They said my superpowers are not
super enough? That's rubbish. I've got loads of
superpowers. I'm overflowing with superpowers.
The school must have made a terrible mistake.
Maybe they got my application mixed up with
somebody else's?'

Mum read a little further down the letter.

'No, Charlie, I don't think so. Look, they've

listed all of your superpowers test results. You failed their flying test. You failed their running test. And you failed their lifting test as well.

Charlie grabbed the letter.

'Let me see . . . Oh, that's not right . . . they've only listed the things that I'm not very good at. Look, there's no mention of my coolest superpowers like my super somersaulting and my super juggling.'

Mum looked at Charlie.

'Dear, I'm not sure that juggling rates very highly as a superpower these days.'

Charlie covered his eyes. 'This is so unfair. All my life I've wanted to go to Super School. There's nothing else that I ever wanted to do. How on earth will I ever get to be a superhero if I don't have any training?'

Mum put her arm round Charlie.

'You know what, maybe this is for the best. Being a superhero is a very, very dangerous job indeed. You have to work long hours. You get cold, you get wet, you get tired. And I've heard that those supervillains can be very rude sometimes.

Perhaps it's time for you to start thinking about choosing a different career. Have you ever considered working in television? I'm sure that you'd make a super game-show host.'

Dad walked over.

'Son, I think what you're experiencing right now can be best described as an important life-learning lesson. In my number-one bestselling book *If You Can Change Your Socks, Then You Can Change the World* I write that a young man's journey through life is very much like taking a walk down a corridor and having to pass through a series of doors. Sometimes when you approach a door it opens for you, but sometimes it doesn't. Charlie, right now you're stuck in front of a door that has the words "Your New Future" written on the front of it. So you know what you have to do to get through that door, Charlie? You have to knock as loudly as you can. Keep knocking and knocking and knocking, until someone finally hears you and opens the door. And if that doesn't work, then try ringing the doorbell instead. Maybe that will get their attention. Do you understand what I'm saying, Charlie? Do you get it?'

'Huh?' Charlie rolled his eyes, looking hopelessly confused.

Trixie glared at her mother.

'So, if Charlie's not going to Super School any more, does that mean that I can't have his room?'

Mum nodded. 'I'm sorry, darling.'

Trixie threw her arms up in disgust. 'Oh, this is the *worst* news ever.'

That night, Charlie with his super night vision shining brightly underneath his blanket, read another of Commander Ron's thrilling stories.

'You wait and see, Commander Ron. One day I'm going to be a superhero just like you. One day people will stop me in the street and say *WOW*. You'll see.'

Charlie closed his book and laid his head down on the pillow.

'And, if that never happens . . . then maybe one day I'll get to give away some really cool prizes on a game show.'

# THE PETRIFYING
# PANT-PLUMMETING
# PLOT

While Charlie slept, hundreds of miles above the Applejack household a sinister dark spaceship slipped into the earth's atmosphere.

On board a short man, dressed from head to toe in black, sat at the controls. The evil maniac known as General Pandemonium looked up briefly as one of his officers approached him holding a small plastic object in his hands.

'General, your doll is ready for inspection.'

General Pandemonium stamped his foot angrily. 'My doll? Lieutenant Kurse, how many times do I have to tell you, they're not called dolls, they're called action figures.'

'Oh, yes – pardon me, sir – your action figure is ready for inspection.'

The general grabbed the miniature version of himself and scrutinised it closely.

His face immediately screwed up. 'No, no, no, no . . . can't you idiots get anything right? This doesn't look anything like me at all. Look at its nose. It's far too big. It looks like a shark's fin glued onto a tennis ball. My nose is nowhere near that size.'

Lieutenant Kurse tried to avoid glaring at the general's enormous nose.

'Um, no, sir. You're right. Your nose is nowhere near that big.'

'And look how short he is. He's an utter shrimp. Oh, this is a complete joke. I asked the designers to turn me into a nasty, evil action figure, and instead they've made me look like an angry midget with a pyramid for a honker.' The general thumped the model's head hard on his desk.

'The kids of today are never going to see me as buff and hip and dangerous if they think that I look like this ninny. It hasn't even got a moustache. Get me a new doll immediately.'

'Um, don't you mean action figure, sir?'

'Yes, yes . . . action figure.'

Lieutenant Kurse saluted the general.

'Oh, and while you're here, Lieutenant, what's the latest with my rap song?'

'Ah, I'm glad you asked. We're just about to release it to every radio station in the world, sir. From what we're hearing it's going to be a *kickin* number-one hit.'

'Good, good . . . And what about my music video?'

'The director is just putting her finishing touches on it as we speak.'

'And how do I look in it? Do I look tall enough? Do I look mean enough?'

'Absolutely. If you looked any tougher you'd probably break the TV screen, sir.'

'Good, good . . .' The general cracked his knuckles and stretched out his small pointy fingers. 'Image is everything, Lieutenant. Gone are the times when you could simply threaten to blow up the world if you wanted to be the galaxy's number-one supervillain. No, no, no . . . nowadays it's all about marketing.'

Just then a loud buzzing noise rang out over the command centre's intercom.

**Earth's atmosphere successfully entered. Radio communications now fully operational.**

The general swivelled round in his seat. 'Okay, now it's time for us to make some headlines.' He pointed at his communications officer. 'Who's in charge of security these days on this stupid planet?'

'Prime Minister Perkins, sir.'

'Right, then, get me Prime Minister Perkins on the line, pronto.'

'Dialling now, sir . . .'

**WHIRR, CLICK, RING.**

'You've reached the Metropolitan Mansion, go ahead, caller . . .'

'This is General Pandemonium speaking . . .'

'I'm sorry, caller, did you say you were a panda?'

'No, no, fool. Listen carefully. My name is General Pan-de-mo-ni-um. I am the world's newest and most deadly supervillain. I demand to speak to the prime minister.'

'Excuse me, Mr, um . . . Panting Gnome . . . but is the prime minister expecting your call?'

'Listen – get me the prime minister on the line right now or I'll have you dipped in a piranha-infested pool of Guzarian juice!'

'Putting you through, now, caller.'

**WHIRR, CLICK, RING.**

'Hi, you've reached the office of Jeffrey Perkins, prime minister and head of world security. I'm

**13**

sorry I can't take your call right now. I'm either away from my desk or doing something else really, really important. But your call means a lot to me – so please leave a message after the beep, and have a nice day.'

**BEEP.**

'Arghh!' The general shook his fist angrily. 'Prime Minister Perkins, my name is General Pandemonium – your new worst nightmare. In forty-eight hours' time I plan to take over your planet. I have at my disposal the most terrifying weapon the world has ever seen. It is called the Undie-taker-downer. When this weapon is fired from space it will disintegrate the elastic fibre and metal attachments in everybody's clothing. Simply put, every pair of pants on the planet will plummet to the ground faster than a falling meteor. Zips will unzip, belts will unclip, and trousers and skirts will implode like collapsing circus tents. Modern civilisation will be sent back to the dark ages as every man, woman and child runs away to hide the embarrassing sight of their exposed bare bottoms.

'In just a few short hours, the people of earth, along with their underwear, will be brought to their knees and left at the mercy of my ruthless control.'

The general arched his eyebrows.

'If you wish to avoid such a global catastrophe you must meet my list of outrageous demands:

'Firstly, I request full control of the world's gold and silver supplies. Secondly, I request full control of the world's diamond reserves. Thirdly, I demand that you allow me to compete on the TV show *I Wanna Be a Rock King* and let me win it. Fourthly, I want the makers of Super Squishy Choco Nuggets to bring back the yellow nugget again. Fifthly, and finally, I wish to have a month of the year named after me. Julius Caesar has July, Emperor Augustus has August, and now I demand that the first month of every year be renamed "Panuary" in my honour. For full terms and conditions on my demands go to my website www.pandemonium-is-da-king.com. There's a link there on the main menu, just below the recipes icon. Oh, and if you think your stupid superheroes are going to save you this time then you're sadly mis—'

**BEEP**.

'Oh, blast, blast . . . The machine's stopped and I haven't finished recording my message yet.'

# A SUPER SECRET

CALLING COMMANDER APPLEJACK. CALLING
COMMANDER APPLEJACK. COME IN COMMANDER
APPLEJACK. THE WORLD NEEDS YOU . . .

Charlie rolled over and hit the snooze button
on his alarm clock. 'I don't think I'll be saving the
world anytime soon . . .' he yawned. He hopped
out of bed, rubbed the sleep from his eyes and
slowly trudged downstairs to the kitchen.

'Good morning, champ,' Dad cried, leaping up
and giving Charlie a way-too-energetic early
morning high five.

Mum dropped two pieces of hot toast on
Charlie's plate.

'Now, dear, remember this is your first day at a

**17**

new school and I don't want you showing off to the other boys and girls. That means no lifting the teachers' cars above your head or creating tidal waves in the swimming pool.'

'I know, I know, Mum. Don't worry, I won't. Nobody's going to know I'm, er, special.

'Son, I've got to hand it to you,' Dad said, smiling. 'You're certainly showing a great attitude about all of this. Listen, I know you'd rather be heading off today to the Super School along with the rest of the other young superheroes – but maybe there's another important life-lesson to be learned here. In my award-winning book *Money Can't Buy You Happiness (But It Can Buy You a Haircut)* I write that people can learn some valuable lessons about happiness from fish. When you place a small fish inside a large bowl it's not very happy because there are so many other larger fish that it has to compete with. However, if you place a large fish inside a small

bowl, it's much happier because there are fewer fish to compete with. So, Charlie, the lesson is this: whatever sized bowl you end up being placed in during your life, always make sure that you act and think like a fish if you want to be happy. Do you know what I mean, son? Do you understand my advice?'

Once again a glazed look came over Charlie's face.

After breakfast, Charlie dragged his feet along the ground and dawdled towards school. 'Oh, this sucks, there won't be any meteor-pulverising lessons where I'm going today . . .'

He kicked a stone high up into the clouds. 'And there won't be any anti-zombie combat training either.'

Charlie went to kick another stone but suddenly he heard a faint cry for help. He closed his eyes and concentrated as hard as he could with his super hearing.

'Call now for the new Turbo Ab burner. Our

red-hot special today is priced at only 99.99 . . .'

Charlie banged his ear and turned in the other direction.

'Help . . . help me . . . Somebody get me down from here!'

He opened his eyes and spotted a schoolboy tied to the top of a rugby goalpost ahead in the distance. He thrust out his arm, superhero style.

'Commander Applejack to the rescue.' He took a few steps but – **KERFLOD** – tripped over his shoes. He jumped up and dusted himself off.

'Commander Applejack to the rescue . . . again.' **WOOSH**.

Charlie rocketed down the street, zipped over a bridge and headed out into the middle of a sports field. He skidded to a halt right underneath the goalposts.

'Help, help, somebody get me down . . .'

'Help has arrived, my friend, and his name is Charlie Applejack.'

The schoolboy stared down in disbelief.

'W-where on earth did you come from?'

'That's not important right now,' Charlie said,

smiling. 'But what *is* important is, who are you? And what are you doing up there?'

'My name's Josh. Josh Eagle. Some bullies put me up here because they didn't like the way I was dressed.'

'They put you up there because they didn't like the way you were dressed?'

'Yeah, they said I looked like my mother still got me ready for school.'

'And what did you say to them?'

'I told them at least I didn't look like I was wearing my mother's clothes – like they did.'

'Oohh, nice comeback line.'

Suddenly a powerful gust of wind rocked the goalposts. 'Hey, can you get me down right away? It's really scary up here.'

Charlie looked around to

make sure nobody was watching. 'No problem . . .
but first I need you to close your eyes.'

'Why?'

''Cause, I get really nervous when somebody
watches me doing something.'

'Oh – okay.' Josh closed his eyes.

Charlie took in a deep breath. 'Up, up and . . . up.'

He launched himself skywards but –

DONGG – smashed into the crossbar and
bounced straight back to the ground.

'Argh!' Josh screamed as the goalposts wobbled
wildly and collapsed, plummeting earthwards.
Charlie quickly rolled onto his back, leapt up and
caught the pole Josh was tied to before it slammed
into the ground.

Josh was gobsmacked.

'H–how did you do that?' he cried.

Charlie shrugged his shoulders. 'Um, I dunno. Lucky catch, I guess.'

'No, no, how did you fly through the air like that?'

Charlie shook his head. 'I didn't fly through the air. I don't know what you're talking about. Anyway, I thought you had your eyes closed?'

Josh smiled. 'Sorry, I peeked.'

Charlie turned bright red. He glanced over his shoulder to check they were still alone.

'Um, Josh, can I let you into a really big secret?'

# ZAP 'EM AND
# WRAP 'EM

'General Pandemonium, we have the Super
School in range, sir. We're ready to neutralise our
objectives.'

'We're ready to what?'

'We're ready to capture the superheroes, sir.'

'Good, Sergeant Briggs. But next time can you
please communicate using plain English. Don't
you read your e-mails? Haven't you heard of our
new command-centre motto K.I.S.S yet? It stands
for "Keep It Simple and Sinister". Remember that,
Sergeant Briggs. It's very important. Now get back
to your station and don't try to confuse me again.'

'Affirmative, sir.'

'What?'

'I mean yes, sir.'

'That's better.'

General Pandemonium parked his spaceship in a position high above the Super School's sports stadium. Below, all of the world's superheroes were gathered together to watch the school's opening-day celebrations. The general could hardly contain his laughter.

'Oh, Lieutenant Kurse, just look at that sight . . . Every single one of the world's superheroes lined up below me like rows and rows of sitting ducks. Oh, it couldn't be easier. In fact, somebody get me a blindfold – at least make my job of capturing them all a little more difficult.'

A loud voice buzzed over the intercom.

**Public address broadcasting system operational.**

General Pandemonium leaned forward and grabbed his microphone. An image of the superheroes flipped up on the viewing screen.

'Superheroes of the world. Greetings. This is General Pandemonium speaking. I want to welcome you all to your doom!'

The general wriggled in his seat with delight. But the superheroes remained motionless. Lieutenant Kurse scratched his head.

'Ah, the superheroes don't seem to be reacting to your threat, sir.'

The general shook his fist. 'Okay, listen up, you stupid superheroes . . . So you think you're tough, do you? Well, let's see how tough you are when I blast you with a force field of Moozem. That's right, I said, Moozem – you know, the stuff that makes you lose your powers and become sicker and weaker than a ninety-year-old school teacher.'

The superheroes still remained motionless.

'Oh, this is a tough audience today, sir. I didn't see a single eyelid bat.'

The fuming general leapt out of his seat. 'I said, you're all doomed – you hear me? DOOMED! DOOMED! DOOMED! DOOMED! DOOMED! DOOMED! Doomed to the power of ten and divided by two. Yes, you sir at the back dressed in the funny green suit pretending not to hear me, you're extra DOOMED!'

Suddenly Lieutenant Kurse received an urgent message in his earpiece. He signalled the general.

'Ah, sir, I think I know why the superheroes aren't reacting to your threats. It seems that we've had a small, er, technical glitch.'

'A technical glitch? What do you mean?'

Lieutenant Kurse gently lifted the general's microphone out of his hands.

'Um, it seems your microphone wasn't switched on, sir.'

He turned the microphone on and handed it back.

'Argh!' The general pounded his head on the desk.

'Okay, we're good to go now. Ah, sir, would you mind repeating everything you've just said?'

The general threw his microphone on the floor and stormed off. 'Oh, forget it. Just zap 'em and wrap 'em.'

**WHIRR, CLUNK.**

**27**

Ten large hatches opened beneath the spaceship. A series of blue lights started pulsing brightly in a repeating pattern.

Suddenly the superheroes leapt to their feet and started cheering.

'I don't believe it,' the general cried. 'They're actually happy about this happening?'

Lieutenant Kurse glanced up at the viewing screen.

'Hmmm, apparently the superheroes have no idea of who we are. I think they believe we're part of the opening celebrations.'

Sergeant Briggs raised his arm.

'Firing the Moozem in three seconds, sir. '

**WOOORONGG.** The spaceship blasted the stadium with a brilliant blue light. The superheroes collapsed in their seats and started shaking violently. General Pandemonium did a little dance.

'Finally, something's working.'

He returned to his seat. 'Make sure the prime minister gets to see these images. Oh, and send him a personal message from me as well. Tell him to have a nice day himself.'

The general swivelled round in his seat and cracked his knuckles. 'Now, with the superheroes out of the way, there's absolutely nobody who can prevent me from unleashing my petrifying pant-plummeting plan! Muhahaha . . .'

Just then a smiling Lieutenant Kurse approached him from behind.

'Ah, sir, I have that blindfold you were asking for . . .'

# CHAOS IN THE CLASSROOM

**RING RING RING RING**. A shrill school bell sounded out in the distance.

Josh looked at his watch. 'Oh no, I can't believe it, I'm going to be late on my first day of school.'

'Let's move it,' Charlie said, turning to run.

'Hey, which class are you in?' Josh cried out, trying to keep up with Charlie.

'Room 23'

'Cool, same as me!'

Later that morning, after the welcoming assembly had finished, Josh and Charlie took their seats in

Room 23 at the back of Mr Frisby's class.

'Psst, Charlie, if you're a superhero, does that mean you're friends with Commander Ron?'

Charlie glared at Josh and placed his finger over his lips. 'Sshhh . . . quiet.'

'Hey, can you bend a lamppost in two with your bare hands, and stop a speeding locomotive with your little finger like Commander Ron can?'

'Josh, I said keep your voice down.'

Mr Frisby's ears pricked up. 'Excuse me, Mr Applejack, but do you have something you want to share with the class?'

Charlie shook his head.

'I'm sure you do. It's obviously *really* important.

Come up to the front and share it with us all . . .'

Charlie looked at Josh, who had slunk down in his seat, and reluctantly went to the front of the class.

'Now, tell us what you and Josh were discussing. I'm sure everyone is dying to know.'

Charlie felt a lump in his throat.

'Um, Josh asked me if I am friends with Commander Ron.'

The class erupted with laughter.

'Oh, and are you friends with Commander Ron?'

Charlie shook his head.

'Um, no.'

'Right . . . and what else did you discuss with Josh?'

'Er, Josh asked if I could bend a lamppost in two with my bare hands and stop a speeding locomotive with my little finger.'

The class erupted again.

'Oh, I see. Well, that certainly sounds very

32

athletic. Tell me, do you think you could bend a lamppost in two with your bare hands, and stop a speeding locomotive with your little finger?'

Charlie blushed. 'Honestly, sir, I'm not really sure . . .'

'What do you mean, you're not really sure?'

'Well, I've never tried it before, sir.'

'Ha-hah-ha!!' The classroom exploded with laughter.

Mr Frisby put his hands on his hips. 'Now listen, Applejack, I enjoy a good story as much as anybody else. In fact when I was your age, I made up a story that I was a superhero too. But you know what, it's the first day of school and I really need you to just sit quietly at your desk and keep your wild and fantastic stories to yourself. I'm sorry to do this on your first day, but in order to teach you a lesson I need you to write for me one hundred times: *I will not interrupt lessons again by making up stories that I am friends with Commander Ron, and wondering whether I can bend a lamppost in two with my bare hands and stop a speeding locomotive with my little finger.*'

Charlie looked at Mr Frisby then walked slowly back to his desk.

'Right, everyone, open your books.'

# CLANG CLANG CLANG CLANG.

Suddenly the school alarm sounded. A loud voice boomed over the classroom speaker.

'Pupils, this is Principal Wilson speaking. I have some terrible news. We have to close school early today and send everyone home.'

'Hooray!' Everybody clapped their hands and whistled.

'Sshhh . . . sshhh . . .' Mr Frisby cried, flapping his arms wildly.

'We've just this moment received news that a deadly new supervillain called General Pandemonium has captured all of the world's superheroes and is holding them as prisoners. He's planning to take over the world and do all sorts of things that are completely against the school rules. I need you to return to your homes as quickly as possible; lock all the doors, listen to your parents,

34

and take good care of your pets . . . That is all for now, children. School dismissed.'

Mr Frisby clapped his hands and stood at the front of the class.

'Okay, people, you heard the principal. This is really serious. Put your books away and let's get moving.'

Josh leaned over to Charlie. 'Hey, at least the news isn't all bad . . .'

'What do you mean?'

'Well, the supervillain didn't catch *all* of the world's superheroes, did he? There's still one roaming free.'

'Who?'

Josh pointed at Charlie. 'You.'

One by one the kids filed out of the classroom. Josh and Charlie were the last to leave. Mr Frisby looked at Charlie as he walked towards the door.

'Ah, Mr Applejack. Now don't forget to do your lines for homework tonight.'

Charlie reached into his back pocket. 'No

problem, sir.' He handed Mr Frisby a thick wad of paper.

'I've already finished them.'

# THE RISE OF THE FALLING TROUSERS

After leaving school together, Josh and Charlie ran back to Josh's house. They rushed into the living room and turned on the TV.

'And now, in breaking news, we take you live to the Metropolitan Trade House with our roving reporter Danny Toopay. Danny . . . are you there? Can you tell us what's happening?'

'Lindsay . . . the prime minister has just lost his underwear. I repeat, the prime minister has just lost his underwear.'

Josh turned up the sound on the TV.

'Danny, can you tell us how this dreadful event happened?'

'Fifteen minutes ago the Metropolitan Trade

House was blasted by a mysterious orange ray from space. Within seconds, the prime minister's trousers tumbled to the ground taking his pants along with them. The deputy prime minister and the visiting president of Finland were hit by this ray as well. Currently, the prime minister is still bottomless as no one can find a pair of pants or trousers to fit him.'

'And what about you, Danny? Are you okay?'

'I'm fine, Lindsay. I felt a strong rumbling around my belt line just a few seconds ago but I think that was the chilli that I had for lunch.'

'Thanks, Danny – we'll cross back to you again in a few minutes' time. Make sure that you and

your pants hang in there . . .'

'Will do, Lindsay.'

Josh looked over at Charlie. 'What on earth is going on?'

'I have no idea.'

Just then Josh's mum jogged into the living room.

'Mum, Mum, you'll never guess what's happened. The prime minister's lost his pants!'

'Really? How terrible. Maybe the deputy prime minister will help him look for them.'

Josh's mum started jumping up and down on the spot. 'Josh, I'd love to stop and talk but I'm right in the middle of a cardio workout. There's some protein bars and health shakes in the fridge for you and your friend if you want them . . .'

'Okay, Mum.'

Charlie looked at Josh. 'What kind of maniac would cause the prime minister's pants to fall down?'

'It must be that madman they were talking about at school – you know, General Pongo Bubblegum, or whatever his name was.'

'So, who is he, and why is he doing this?'
Charlie cried.

Josh switched off the TV. 'I don't know, but let's find out.'

Josh and Charlie jogged up the stairs into Josh's bedroom. Josh turned on his computer and clicked on his favourite Internet search page.

'We need to find some background information on this guy,' Charlie said. 'Try searching on *evil villain*.'

Josh tapped the keyboard. 'How do you spell villain? Is it with one l or two?'

'Two.'

Josh shook his head.

'Nope – nothing informative here. What else could we try?'

'How about *evil madman*?'

Josh tapped the keyboard again. 'Nope. Nothing detailed here either.'

Charlie looked at the screen. 'Okay . . . just try something ridiculous like *baddy*.'

Josh ran his fingers over the keys.

'Hey, wait a minute. Yep – there's a link here to his official web page. The address is www.pandemonium-is-da-king.com.' Josh clicked on the link. 'Okay, his name is General P. D. Pandemonium. He's a graduate from the Intergalactic Academy of Mayhem. He started off his criminal career as Corporal Punishment; then he became Major Panic; and now he's promoted himself to a general. His goals are world domination, global suffering, and to be seen as a positive role model for all young criminals.'

'The guy's a freakazoid,' Charlie said.

Josh peered at the screen. 'Wow, check out the size of his nose. He could poke out somebody's eye with that thing.'

Charlie leaned over and scrolled down the screen. He clicked on a link just below the recipes icon.

'Whoa – check this out: in twenty-four hours' time we're all going to be pantless!'

'What?' Josh peered desperately at the screen.

'The general has a super weapon called the

Undie-taker-downer and he's going to fire it at earth tomorrow. It's going to take down every pair of pants on the planet.'

'No way,' Josh cried. I've got my skateboarding champs tomorrow. I can't possibly ride in them if my bum's on display.'

Charlie scrolled further down the screen. He came across a sight that took his breath away.

'Commander Ron . . . Oh, I can't look, this is too horrible.'

On the screen was a video image of Commander Ron lying on the ground. 'Help me, somebody help me,' he moaned.

'What's wrong with him?' Josh cried. 'He's lying there like some deflated beach ball. And look at the other superheroes – they're all crying and dribbling. Where on earth are they?'

Charlie zoomed in on the image. 'They're at the Super School. I'd recognise that place any day. The general's keeping them hostage in the sports stadium.'

He clenched his fist. 'This is disgusting. No one disrespects Commander Ron like that. General

Pandemonium's gone too far.
Someone's got to stop him.
Someone's got to put him
away for good.'

'Right, so when are you
going to get started?' Josh said.

'Me?' Charlie cried.

Josh kung fu kicked a pillow.
'Yeah, you. What are you
going to do first? Are you
going to knock him out with
a super punch . . . or are you
going to melt him down to his
boots with your super heat vision?'

'Josh, listen, I haven't done any training. I don't
even know how to fly properly. I'm not a real
superhero yet.'

Josh looked at his watch.

'Okay, well, we've got just under a day to turn
you into one!'

# THE PLUMMETING PANTS PENALTY BOX PILE-UP

'General Pandemonium.'

'Yes, what is it, Lieutenant Kurse?'

'I have some news for you, sir.'

'Oh, is it good news?'

Lieutenant Kurse nodded.

'Excellent, I love good news. How wonderful.'

'Um, but, sir, I also have some bad news as well . . .'

The general slammed his fist on the table. 'Lieutenant Kurse, how many times do I have to tell you – never give me good news followed by bad news. I forbid it.'

Lieutenant Kurse paused for a moment.

'O-okay, sir . . . would you rather I gave you a little bit of bad news followed by more bad news instead?'

'No, no, no. That's not the point.' The general stared at the lieutenant and sighed. 'Never mind. What is it, then?'

'Sir, the good news is that your rap song "Global Rage" is the number one most downloaded song in Japan.'

'Wonderful!' The general let out a whoop and grinned at his crew. 'Number one! Did you hear that everyone? I'm number one!'

'In Japan, yes. But, sir, the kids are going absolutely nuts over your song. It's being played in schools, department stores, restaurants, prisons and even out on oil rigs.'

The general leaned back in his chair and kissed the back of his gloved hand. 'Number one . . .' he whispered again. Suddenly he swivelled round. 'Now tell me the bad news.'

'Um, sir . . . Prime Minister Perkins said that he can't meet all of your demands.'

'What? Why ever not?'

'H–he's having problems with the gold and silver supplies, sir. Apparently the miners are on strike and nobody is returning his calls. He asked if you would consider taking bronze instead? There's plenty of that in stock at the moment. Also there's been a slight hiccup with the yellow squishy nuggets.'

'What sort of hiccup?'

'Um, the head chef at Super Squishy has lost the recipe. He can't quite remember how he used to make them.'

General Pandemonium gripped the portable firing controls of the Undie-taker-downer.

'Hmmm . . . I think the prime minister needs a little extra motivation to meet my demands. Perhaps a swift "kick" in the pants will do the trick.' A target grid popped up on the viewing screen. 'I'm about to launch a surprise attack that will send shockwaves around the world.'

Lieutenant Kurse looked at the general. 'Sir, you're not going to fire the Undie-taker-downer at the World Banking Headquarters are you?'

The general shook his head. 'No.'

'Oh, surely not the Hoogenheimer Centre where they're holding the global peace talks?'

'No, no, Lieutenant. I'm going to choose a target that's far more important.'

The viewing screen flickered brightly for a moment and the image of two teams playing soccer appeared in the middle of the target grid. 'I'm going to destroy the World Continental Cup semi-final between the Euro All Stars and Team Americas with a shocking pant-plummeting disaster.'

A quiet hush fell over the command centre. The general smiled menacingly.

'The quickest way to throw the planet into utter chaos is to stop a game of football!'

He puffed out his chest. 'Finally, the time has come for the world to sit up and take notice of who I am. Finally, the people will realise just how vile, nasty and merciless I can really be. Oh, yes . . . nobody's gonna want to mess with me after this. Yeah, I'm going to be feared all over the galaxy.'

**BING-BONG**. Suddenly a soft voice echoed over the intercom.

'General Pandemonium, your poodle groomers have arrived, sir. They're ready to give Miffy Wiffy her shampoo and pedicure.'

'No, no, no. Not now!' barked General Pandemonium. 'Can't you see I'm busy being evil and ruthless? Tell them to come back in ten minutes.'

'Very well, sir.'

The general placed his finger on the firing button.

'All right, World Cup football players, it's time to say goodbye to your pants – or as they say in Japan, where I'm number one, *Sayonara, pantos*.'

# BEWARE THE BULLY-BASHING BOGEY

'Charlie, when I kick my right leg out, that means I want you to fly to the right, okay?'

'Um, okay, I suppose.'

Charlie, holding on to the back of Josh's kite, looked down at his friend nearly fifteen metres below him.

'Josh, do you really think this is the best way to learn to fly? What happens if I fall from here? I'm a long way up.'

'You'll be fine. Just don't let go of my kite.'

Josh pulled the kite strings hard and kicked out his right leg. But Charlie didn't move.

'Hey – what's wrong?' Josh looked up. 'Have

you got your eyes closed or something?'

Charlie quickly re-opened his eyes. 'No, no. I was just protecting them from the wind.'

'Okay, let's do it. On the count of three. One . . . two . . . three . . .'

Charlie took a deep breath and rolled to his right. Josh yanked the kite strings hard into his chest, sending Charlie barrelling through the air in a series of powerful twisting turns.

'Arghhh . . .' Charlie gripped Josh's kite tightly as the wind whipped his face and stung his ears. Josh guided Charlie round in a giant looping circle, then hovered him back up over his head again.

'How cool was that?' Josh cried.

'I feel airsick,' Charlie groaned.

'Okay, now let's try something really tricky this time.' Josh flicked out his left leg.

'Wait . . . wait,' Charlie cried. 'I can't feel my fingers any more.'

Just then, a loud, threatening voice boomed across the park.

'Hey, look – if it isn't the little baby whose mummy still dresses him.'

Josh froze. It was Adam and Zac Skiff, the two bullies who had strung him up on the goalposts earlier that day. Charlie, hiding behind Josh's kite, watched from above, unnoticed by the Skiff brothers.

'I thought the principal told everyone to stay indoors,' Adam cried.

'Yeah, it's not safe being out here. It could be very, *very* dangerous for your health,' Zac chipped in.

Josh took a few steps backwards.

'Back off, you big apes. Listen, I'm friends with a superhero. If you even try and look at me the wrong way, he'll fly down here and crush you like eggshells.'

'Oh, is that so? Well, I don't see him rushing to help you. Anyway, haven't you heard the news? There are no superheroes left any more. They've all been captured by an evil supervillain. Good job too. So, I guess you're right out of luck, loser.'

'Stop – I'm warning you.' Josh looked up at Charlie. 'My friend will be here any second.'

'Oh yeah?' Zac and Adam moved in.

Josh desperately tugged the kite strings. 'I said he'll be here *any* second.'

Adam grabbed Josh's collar and lifted him off the ground. Suddenly Charlie let go of the kite and dived through the air. He rocketed down towards the bullies but – THOCK – smashed into a tree branch.

'Arghhh!' He tumbled down through the tree and ended up landing head first in a rubbish bin.

'Um, are you sure that guy's really a superhero? He looks more like a superzero to me,' Zac said, sneering.

Charlie jumped to his feet, with the bin stuck
tightly on his head and rubbish streaming down
his front.

'Okay, mummy's boy, where do you want us to
string you up this time?' said Zac.

'How about the lamppost?' Adam suggested. 'I
hear it has a great view.'

'No, no . . . leave me alone!'

Inside the rubbish bin, Charlie felt an itching
sensation in his nose. His nostrils
throbbed and burned
with the smell
of onions. '**AA-
AA . . .
AA . . .
ACHOO**!!' Charlie
blew the rubbish bin
apart with a super
sneeze. Apple cores
and soggy tomatoes
hurtled through the air
and – **KERSPLAT** –
the bullies were suddenly

covered from head to toe in stinky, slimy gunk.

'Ewwwgh!' Adam wiped a peanut-butter sandwich off his face.

'**AA-AA . . . ACHOO!**' Charlie erupted with another super sneeze, knocking Zac off his feet with a flying bogey.

'C'mon – run!' Adam cried.

Josh let out a whoop as the bullies scurried away. He patted Charlie on the back. 'Awesome . . . work my man. You literally blew them away with your super sneeze.'

Charlie smiled and picked potato skins out of his hair.

'So, Charlie, not a bad day's training, eh? Today

you learned how to take off, fly, and land – well, crash land – and now you know how to blow away the bad guys. I think you're ready to save the world next.'

Charlie was quiet for a moment.

'There's just one problem though,' he said. 'I'm not sure if my mum will let me.'

# THE AGE OF GLOBAL RAGE

'Mum, Dad, I need to ask you something really important.'

Charlie awkwardly shuffled his feet. 'Um, would it be okay if I went out with my friend Josh and tried to save the world . . .'

Suddenly Trixie burst into the kitchen. Her face was screwed up like a squeezed lemon. She was holding her cat Mr Tiddlebink in her arms.

'Help. Help. It's a disaster! Somebody help me . . .'

'Trixie – what's wrong, sweetheart?' Mum cried.

'Is there a fire? A flood? An earthquake?' shouted Dad.

Trixie grabbed both her mum and dad and

dragged them into the lounge. She tearfully pointed at the television. 'My favourite TV programme's not on any more. I was right in the middle of watching *Radical Pet Makeover* and the stupid screen went blank.'

Mum and Dad looked at each other.

'Now I don't know how to finish braiding the hair extensions on Mr Tiddlebink's tail. It's an absolute disaster.'

Mum hugged Trixie. 'It'll be all right, sweetie, we'll find a way to fix Mr Tiddlebink's tail.'

Dad bent down and adjusted the controls on the TV.

'Hmmm, that's strange. Every other channel is blank too. I wonder if there's a problem with our reception?'

Suddenly the screen flickered into life. A ghostly image appeared through the fog of static. It was a short man with an enormous nose dressed all in black.

'Greetings, people of the world, I am General Pandemonium, the galaxy's most sensational new supervillain. You might remember me from

such outrageous disasters as the plunging of the prime minister's pants and the shocking World Cup penalty box pants-down pile-up. In less than three hours' time I plan to unleash a new terror on your planet – the likes of which you have never witnessed before. But this global calamity can be avoided if your petty prime minister will only agree to meet my demands. Prime Minister Perkins, if you are watching, act now . . . or else face your certain doom!'

The general disappeared from the screen, then reappeared wearing sunglasses.

'And now for your viewing entertainment, I'm proud to present you with the world-wide premiere of the music video for my rap song "Global Rage".'

The screen flooded with swirling colours and a thumping bass line pounded through the speakers.

'Burn the page . . . shake your cage . . . dis – en – gage . . . *GLOBAL RAGE*!'

Mum covered her ears and walked away. Trixie jumped up and down, singing along to the song. Mr Tiddlebink sniffed at his half-braided tail.

Dad looked over at Charlie. 'Hey, son, you've got to hand it to those TV guys, they certainly know how to boost their ratings. Boy oh boy, everybody's going to be tuned in tonight to see what happens at the end of this programme.'

'Dad, Dad . . . this is not a TV stunt. This guy really is a supervillain. He's wants to take over the world.'

'Really? How's he going to do it?'

'He's going to make everybody's underpants fall down by destroying the elastic in our clothing. We're all going to be pantless in a few hours' time.'

'Oh my word. Is that really true?'

'Dad, it's the honest truth. I wouldn't lie about something as important as our pants.'

Mum looked over at Dad.

'Dear, I think we're all worrying about absolutely nothing at all. Listen, even if he makes our pants fall down, we can still get along just fine without them. The Roman Empire never had pants, and they did pretty well for themselves. And so did the Vikings – they were pantless but highly productive.'

Dad pushed his glasses up his nose.

'Darling – I hear what you're saying, but I'm not sure that I totally agree with you. You do realise that if all the elastic in our clothing is destroyed, then there'll be no tennis any more?'

'What?'

'Well, how are you going to play your interclub final on Sunday if your skirt doesn't stay up when you go to serve the ball?'

Mum's face dropped. 'Oh – this is outrageous! This maniac must be dealt with immediately.'

Charlie stood up.

'Mum, Dad, I want to ask your permission to save the world. I want to stop General Pandemonium and I want to save our pants.'

'Well, I guess, maybe just this once, you can,' Mum said doubtfully. 'But only if you take your father's mobile phone with you so that we can call you if we need to. Oh, and do make sure that you put on something nice, dear. I don't want you going out in that scruffy old sweatshirt you always wear. There might be cameras around.'

Charlie smiled. 'No problem, Mum.'

# THE TRICYCLE OF TERROR

'Hey, Charlie,' Josh said, opening the door to his house. 'What did your mum say?'

Charlie gave Josh the thumbs up.

'Brilliant! Okay, let's go and do battle with the general.' Josh grabbed his jacket and slipped on his trainers.

'So, where's your superhero costume?'

Charlie looked blank. 'My superhero costume? I don't have one.'

'What? You're about to go head to head with the world's deadliest supervillain and you don't have a costume? That's ridiculous: you gotta have one. Wait here.'

Josh sprinted up the stairs. Thirty seconds later

he returned holding a box under his arm.

'Okay, put these on.' Josh handed Charlie a pair of yellow gloves and what looked like a blue cape. Charlie sniffed the gloves.

'Hey, these are cleaning gloves. And this isn't a cape, it's a shower curtain.'

Josh smiled.

'It's the best I could do in the time that I had.'

Josh then placed a swimming cap and some goggles over Charlie's head.

'What are those for?'

'To protect your secret identity. With the goggles on you're a mysterious superhero. With the goggles off you're just plain old Charlie Applejack. Plus the swimming cap will keep your head warm when you're flying.'

Charlie stood in front of the mirror looking at his costume.

'So, what do you think?' asked Josh.

Charlie frowned. 'I smell of lavender and lemon.'

Josh bent down to tie up his laces. 'Oh, and there's one more important thing you need.'

'What's that?'

'You need to give yourself a superhero name. Have you got any good ideas?'

Charlie paused in thought. 'Hey, I know – how about Captain Responsible? I've got a very responsible job to do.'

Josh laughed out loud. 'Captain Responsible? Are you serious? That sounds more like someone who's in charge of a school crossing-guard patrol. No, no, you need a name that's big, strong and powerful. Something that will strike fear into the heart of a supervillain.'

Charlie pursed his lips. 'Um, I know, how about – Commander Big, Strong and Powerful?'

'Uh.' Josh slapped his forehead. 'This is going to be much harder than I thought.'

He glanced at his watch. 'Listen, we're running out of time – just think of something short and punchy.'

'Sure thing.' Charlie puffed out his chest. 'How about . . . Hero Boy?'

Josh looked at Charlie. 'Okay, Hero Boy it is.'

Charlie moved towards the door and thrust out his arm. 'Hero Boy to the rescue.'

Josh tapped him on the shoulder. 'Ah, aren't you forgetting someone?'

'Oh, yeah.' Charlie thrust out his arm again. 'Hero Boy and *Josh* to the rescue.'

The two boys jogged down the stairs and ran out into the front garden.

Charlie looked around. 'Okay – we need to find some transport to get us to the Super School.'

'Transport?' asked Josh. 'I thought you were our

transport – aren't you going to fly us there?'

Charlie rubbed his already twice-bashed forehead. 'Ummm. I don't think my head could take it. Do you know how many trees there are between here and the Super School?'

'So how else are we going to get there? By bus?'

'How about this?' Charlie said, pointing to his left.

Josh's eyebrows arched. 'My little sister Bindy's tricycle? Are you crazy?'

'No, no, listen, Josh. It's perfect. Look, we can both ride on it.'

Charlie jumped onto the tricycle's seat. 'C'mon, let's get going – there's no time to lose.'

Josh reluctantly hopped down behind him.

'This is not how I imagined I'd be leaving to save the world . . .'

SCREECH. Charlie blasted off on the tricycle leaving three smoking skid marks on the driveway. He put his head down and furiously pedalled away.

Suddenly a police siren sounded.

'Pull over!' a voice boomed over a loudspeaker.

'Charlie – we've got company.'

Charlie looked over his shoulder. The police officer flashed his lights and radioed for help. Charlie listened in with his super hearing.

'Attention all units, this is Red Five. I'm in hot pursuit of an unidentified vehicle travelling out of the city towards the Furlington Hills at ten times the speed limit. I'm requesting back-up.'

'Roger that, Red Five. Can you give us a description of the vehicle, please?'

'Sure thing . . . it's a low-slung, pink, three-wheeler vehicle, with two male occupants on board. Its registration number is B–I–N–D–Y.'

'Roger that, Red Five. We're joining in the chase.'

Suddenly two more police sirens sounded.

'Charlie, hurry,' urged Josh. 'You gotta get us out of here. I don't want to be arrested for speeding on my sister's tricycle!'

'No problemo.'

Charlie took a huge breath and pumped his legs like nuclear-powered pistons. They shot forward at the speed of sound, leaving the police cars standing. Josh felt his stomach turn inside out as the tricycle thundered over a hump-backed bridge and flew through the air, landing a fifty metres down the road.

A few minutes later the noisy sirens faded into the background as the police gave up the chase.

Charlie looked over his shoulder.

'So how was that for a getaway?' he asked.

Josh, turning whiter than chalk, tried to stop his teeth from chattering.

'Ch-Ch-harlie, how about n-next time we t-take the b-bus?'

# 11

# BREAKING THE BAD NEWS

'*Burn the page . . . shake your cage . . . dis – en – gage . . . GLOBAL RAGE!*'

General Pandemonium leapt about the command centre with his song blaring at eardrum-bursting levels. He spun in a circle, then began gliding smoothly backwards across the shiny floor. Just at that moment Lieutenant Kurse entered the room.

'General Pandemonium, excuse me, sir?'

The general tripped and fell. Lieutenant Kurse dived forward and grabbed him just before he hit the floor.

'Let go of me, you fool – I meant to do that.'

The general sprung back to his feet. 'So,

Lieutenant, what did you think of my new dance move? Pretty cool, eh? I'm thinking of calling it the moonwalk. You see, you slide your feet backwards like this, and it makes you look like you're walking on the moon.'

'Ah, very clever, sir . . . but I think somebody else has already invented the moonwalk . . .'

'Nonsense, I'm the first person to think of it. It's my idea. Boy, the kids are going to dig this move.' The general returned to his seat. 'Now, Lieutenant, why are you here?'

'I have the new designs for your action figures, sir.' The lieutenant opened a bag and pulled out some small plastic figurines.

The general's eyes lit up.

'Ohhh. Yes, much better. They all look positively evil. And, look at this little chappy with the horrible scar on his cheek. How lovely.'

'Ah, yes sir, he's the High Seas Pirate version of you, sir. He's most impressive . . . and quite intimidating too.' The lieutenant shuffled through the other action figures. 'We also have you appearing as a Kung Fu Fighter, a Deadly Commando, and my personal favourite, sir, the Fearless Hawaiian Firewalker. Look, he even comes with his very own plastic imitation firestones.'

'Ooohh.' The general grabbed the figurine and started playing with it.

'Danger, danger . . . stay away from those firestones . . . Hah, have no fear, General Pandemonium's here, his toes are tougher than titanium . . .'

The general handed back the model to the lieutenant.

'Very good.' He paused for a moment. 'Okay, now what's your bad news?'

73

'My bad news, sir?'

'Yes, Lieutenant, you always give me good news followed by bad news. So out with it, then.'

The lieutenant shrugged his shoulders. 'Nope, nothing to report at the moment, sir.'

'Really? Not even a whisper?'

The lieutenant nodded. 'Not a smidgen.'

Suddenly an alarm sounded. Lieutenant Kurse's facial muscles tightened.

The general leapt to his feet. 'What is going on?' he cried.

The lieutenant took a deep breath. 'Ah, sir, I'm sure it's nothing to worry about. Um, it's probably just a drill. It'll be over in a few seconds.'

The alarm grew louder. Lieutenant Kurse received an urgent message in his earpiece. His pulse raced.

'Ummm, sir, you'll never believe it, but I've just received some . . . baaa . . . er, um, some *breaking* news.'

The general glared at the lieutenant. 'What sort of breaking news?'

'Sir, it appears that an unidentified object is

rapidly approaching our position at the Super
School.'

'ARGHHH!!!! Lieutenant, this isn't breaking
news – this is bad news!'

'Perhaps a little on the baddish side . . .'

'Okay, who, what and where is this thing?'

'Ah, I'm sorry, but the object's too small to scan,
sir. We've no way of knowing if there are any
intelligent life forms on board.'

'Right – I'm not taking any chances with this
one. I'm going down there to sort this problem out
myself.' He raised his arm. 'Sergeant Briggs, I want
you to release my STINK-R.'

Sergeant Briggs did a double-take.

'You really want me to release your Special
Tactical Intelligent Nuclear Killer-Robot?'

The general nodded. 'Yes I do, Sergeant.
Nothing is going to stop me from conquering the
world. My giant STINK-R will make sure of that!'

# 12

# iT'S PANDEMONiUM!

After ten more minutes of furious pedalling
Charlie came to a strange-looking roundabout
and took the first exit – a steep track marked
'No Public Access'. When he reached the top of
the track he skidded to a halt and leapt off the
tricycle. Josh, still feeling dizzy, jumped off behind
him. Smoke rose from the battered tricycle's tyres.

'Okay, prepare to be blown away,' warned
Charlie. 'You've never seen anything as cool as
this.'

Josh squinted. 'What? All I can see is the top of
a dusty old hill. Where's the Super School? Is it
hidden behind an invisible wall or something?'

Charlie grinned and pointed to the crest of the
hill.

'Check it out.'

Josh walked over to the edge and looked down into the valley below.

'Huh? All I can see is some cows . . . two ducks . . . and an old fence.'

Charlie ran to join him. 'What? Don't tell me we're . . . we must be up the wrong hill. Oh no, we should be on top of that other hill over there.' Josh and Charlie sprinted back to the tricycle.

'C'mon, Charlie, hurry, we've only got fifteen minutes left before our pants get zapped.'

Charlie roared furiously away.

'Sorry about that. The last time I came here my dad did all the driving.'

Charlie barrelled back to the strange roundabout, took the second exit – another steep track marked 'No Public Access' – then rocketed up to the top of the next hill. He screeched to a standstill and jumped off the tricycle. Josh hopped off, sniffing the air.

'Something's burning. Hey, look, all the tyres have melted.'

Charlie glanced down. 'Oops. I think your sister might notice that her trike seems lower to the ground than it was the last time she rode it.'

'No worries,' Josh said. 'I'll just tell her she must be getting taller.'

Josh and Charlie ran over to the edge. Josh stared into the valley beneath. His eyes bulged like tennis balls.

'Whoa! That's the Super School? You're kidding me. It looks more like the world's most amazing adventure park.'

Charlie smiled. 'I know, it's pretty cool, eh?'

'Wow, I wish our school was like that.'

Charlie sighed. 'Tell me about it . . .'

Josh looked around. 'Okay, so how do we get into the school? Is there a secret tunnel? A super-strong gate with a password lock? Or, I know, I bet we have to have our eyes scanned by some high-tech X-ray machine?'

'Nah,' Charlie said. 'You just follow that path

over there; the one with the sign that says "This way to the Super School".'

'Oh.'

Charlie and Josh sprinted down a long path that led them out into the middle of a wide open field.

'Huh, you'd think the groundsman would take better care of the school fields than this, wouldn't you?' Josh exclaimed in disgust. 'Look at those huge potholes over there; they look like bomb craters – they're big enough to drive a bus into.'

'You do know this is where they do the meteor-pulverising training?' Charlie said.

'Oh, really? Well, we'd better not hang around, then.' Josh anxiously looked skyward and started to run.

Charlie led him up a hill towards an oddly shaped concrete building surrounded by high barbed-wire fences and plastered with warning signs.

'What's inside there?' Josh said. 'Is it something top secret?'

'No, it's just the school pool.' Charlie said.

'The school pool? Then what's with all the

security? Are they worried that someone might break in and go swimming without asking permission?'

'Um, no, there's no risk of that happening. The six different species of killer sharks in the pool would make sure of that.'

'Ah . . .' Josh said, raising his eyebrows.

'All right, let's keep moving,' Charlie said, jogging away.

A few minutes later, the two boys reached the heart of the Super School and hid behind a sign.

'So, Charlie, where did you say the general's keeping the superheroes?'

'In the sports stadium.'

'Where's that?'

Charlie raised his arm. 'Over there, to the left of that volcano.'

'V-volcano? The Super School has a volcano?'

'Sure does. They imported it specially to use for their disaster prevention programme. It also supplies the school with heating in winter.'

Josh smiled. 'Now, that's seriously eco-friendly.'
He strained his eyes and looked to the left of the
volcano. 'Oh, wait, I think I can see the sports
stadium. Is it that black building with the big
cloud above it?'

Charlie stared closely at the sports stadium with
his super vision.

'Um, Josh, that's no cloud.'

'What?'

'It's General Pandemonium's spaceship.'

Josh gulped. 'That's not good, is it?'

Charlie scanned the ground below the spaceship
to check for any sign of activity.

'So, how exactly do the two of us take on a
spaceship?' Josh asked.

'Hmmm, well, I guess surrounding it is out of the question,' Charlie said, adjusting his goggles.

Josh looked at Charlie. 'We need the other superheroes to help us.'

Charlie nodded. 'It's our only chance – we've got to set them free or else we're history.'

Josh and Charlie left their hiding place and ran towards the simmering volcano. They ran past the smouldering lava flows and zigzagged through a series of gigantic trees until finally they reached the grounds of the sports stadium.

Suddenly Charlie doubled over as he felt a stabbing pain in his stomach.

'What's wrong?' Josh cried.

'I dunno.'

Josh grabbed Charlie's arm and helped him back to his feet.

'I think there might be some Moozem around here.'

'Moozem? What's Moozem?' asked Josh.

'I read about it on the Internet. It's some

new chemical substance that superheroes have no defence against. It saps you of all your superpowers. It's also supposed to give you really bad wind . . .' Charlie pointed at the spaceship. 'That must be how the general's keeping the superheroes trapped. He's found some Moozem.'

'So how are we going to rescue the superheroes if you're affected by the Moozem as well?'

'I have no idea,' Charlie admitted.

Suddenly – **KA-BOOM** – a giant metallic foot slammed down from the sky behind Josh and Charlie.

'Run!' Josh tugged Charlie's arm and pulled him away. The two boys staggered to their right and dived behind a bush.

Josh peered through the branches. He saw a short man dressed in black sitting on top of a huge hulking metallic robot.

He turned to Charlie. 'I think it's General Pandemonium!'

# THE ATTACK OF THE DEADLY STINK-R

**KA-BOOM!** The giant foot slammed down again, shaking the ground like an earthquake. Charlie peered through a gap in the leaves.

'Man, look at the size of that thing.'

'I know,' Josh whispered. 'I've never seen a nose that big before.'

'No, no, I mean the robot. Look, it's ginormous. How on earth are we going to get past it?'

'What do you mean *we*? You're the one with the superpowers. Aren't you going to knock it out with a super karate chop?'

'Are you kidding? That thing's ten times bigger than me. It'll swat me like a fly.'

'Hey, I know – maybe you could blast it off its

feet with a super sneeze?'

Suddenly a loud voice boomed across the courtyard.

'Give yourselves up now, dirtbags – or face your doom. Resistance is futile.'

General Pandemonium grabbed his laser viewfinder and scanned the bushes. 'Surrender this instant or I will release my deadly STINK-R on you.'

Josh and Charlie refused to budge.

The general looked at his watch. 'All right, have it your way, then ... but it's your funeral, not mine. Prepare to be obliterated by the world's most sophisticated fighting machine.' He switched on his microphone and adjusted his headset.

'STINK-R, crush the intruders.'

'*Beep-affirmative.*' The giant robot lunged towards Charlie and Josh, but suddenly turned left and ran towards the sports stadium.

**KERASH**. It smashed a huge hole in the middle of the two front doors.

'*Beep-STINK-R-crash-into-two-doors . . .*'

'No STINK-R. I didn't say crash into two doors

– I said *crush the intruders*.' The general grabbed his communicator and paged the spaceship above him.

'Lieutenant Kurse, there's a problem with the STINK-R's voice recognition system. Its brain must be even smaller than yours. Fix it now!'

'Ah, sorry, sir, I'd love to help, but I can't. The technician's out on his lunchbreak having a massage. Um, have you tried giving it a bang, sir – that might work.'

'A bang? Lieutenant, are you telling me that I've spent fifteen billion space dollars on the world's most advanced weaponry system, and that I have to give it a bang to make it work properly?'

'It's worth a try, sir.'

'Arghh . . .' The general clenched his fist and banged the robot's head hard.

'*Beep-ouch-STINK-R-catch-two-intruders*.'

The killer robot reversed out of the stadium and charged towards Charlie and Josh's position. It stopped ten feet short of them and focused its red laser beam on a tall tree. *KERZAM*. A scorching bolt of energy cut the tree in half. The robot

turned a few degrees to its right and lit up the
bush Charlie and Josh were hiding behind with a
deep red glow.

'Charlie, do something,' Josh cried. But Charlie
wasn't there, he had disappeared.

# 14

# A TRULY TREACHEROUS TEST

Something grabbed Josh's foot and pulled him away from the bush.

**KERZAM.** The bush exploded in a ball of flames.

'Charlie, where are you? Don't leave me,' Josh wailed.

'Josh, don't worry – I'm right here.'

'Where?' Josh poked out his finger.

'Oww, that was my eye!'

'Charlie – you've turned invisible.'

'What?'

'You're totally see-through.'

Charlie held his hand up. 'Wow – this must be some sort of super reaction to being in life-threatening danger.'

'You mean, you didn't know you could turn invisible?'

'No . . . and I've never been in life-threatening danger before either. Hey, this will come in really handy the next time I get detention.'

**KA-BOOM**. The robot thundered closer.

'Charlie, we gotta do something now or else we're dead meat.'

Charlie furrowed his invisible brow. 'Okay, I've got it. I'll creep up behind the robot and knock out General Pandemonium before he sees me coming. You run through the hole in the sports stadium doors and start dragging out the superheroes.'

'Okay.'

Charlie jumped to his feet and quietly tiptoed across the grass. He crept up behind the robot but suddenly da-da-da - ding-ding-ding . . . his mobile phone rang. Charlie turned red with embarrassment, instantly losing his invisibility.

'Son, it's Dad calling. We're just checking in to see if you're doing all right.'

'Dad, I can't talk – there's a ten-metre killer

robot about to crush me . . .'

'I'm sorry to hear that, son . . . but just think of this as another one of those important life-learning lessons. In my book *The Bigger They Are, The Harder They*—'

Charlie snapped the phone shut.

**KA-BOOM**. The giant robot swivelled round. General Pandemonium glared down at him.

'Who on earth do you think you are? And what is that ridiculous costume you are wearing?'

Charlie raised his hand high above his head.

'Stop – I arrest you in the name of the, um, prime minister!'

'Ha-hah-ha!' General Pandemonium rocked in his seat with laughter. 'Excuse me, are you for real? Is this some sort of practical joke? Where are the hidden cameras?'

'I said stop or I'll—'

A snake-like arm shot out from the robot's side

and grabbed Charlie's wrist. **WOOSH**. It yanked him skywards and started spinning him round in circles.

'Argh!' Charlie felt his eyeballs rattle in his head like marbles in a mixer. General Pandemonium leaned over to look at Charlie's costume.

'Hmmm. Is that a shower curtain you're wearing? And are those yellow rubber gloves?'

He pushed a button and Charlie's body stopped spinning. Charlie groaned weakly, feeling too dizzy to talk.

'Listen, you annoying little pest, I'm just a few minutes away from achieving evil history – and

I'm not going to let a twit like you get in the way.' The general flipped a switch. 'Prepare to be vaporised.'

'Nooo!!!' Josh jumped out from behind the bush. 'Leave him, alone you big-nosed bully.'

The general looked

down in disgust. 'What? There's two of them?'

A second snake-like arm shot out and grabbed Josh round the neck, yanking him up in the air.

'Let me go . . . you don't know who you're dealing with. My f-friend is a superhero.'

The arm lifting Josh stopped.

'I'm sorry, did you say your friend was a superhero?'

'Yeah. He's Hero Boy. Any minute now he's going to break free and pound you like a pancake.'

'Oh really? How exciting. Unfortunately, I've never heard of him. What's his superhero name again?'

Josh tried to loosen the arm's grip round his neck.

'H-his name is Hero Boy. What's yours - Cloth Ears?'

'Hero Boy?' The general laughed out loud. 'Huh, more like *Zero Boy*. Now, listen, squirt, don't take this personally, but I find it very hard to believe that your little friend is a superhero. Anyone who walks around in broad daylight wearing goggles and a swimming cap is in need of serious help if you ask me. But don't just take my word for it. Let's run a little test to find out if he really is a superhero or not.'

'A test? What sort of test?'

'This test.'

The general pushed a button and – **WOOSH** – Charlie was launched into the air and out into the middle of the Moozem force field that covered the sports stadium.

'Say hello to the other superheroes from me,' the general cried, preening his moustache.

# A GUST OF GAGGING GAS

'Help me . . . somebody help me . . .'

Charlie's ears pricked up. It sounded like Commander Ron. He rolled onto his front.

'Commander Ron, I can help you. I'm coming!'

Charlie staggered weakly to his feet. He clasped his stomach tightly as he felt a burning sensation from the effects of the Moozem. Gritting his teeth, he stumbled out into the centre of the sports stadium.

'Help, somebody help me . . .'

Charlie spotted the world's greatest superhero lying face down in the dirt, dribbling like a baby.

'Commander Ron, I'm Charlie Applejack. I'm your greatest fan. Sir, I'm here to rescue you.

Just tell me what to do. Just say a word. Just say
anything . . .'

**ÞHRRRRRRRRRRAAAAAAÞÞÞÞÞ**.

A giant gust of gas that smelt like a thousand rotten

eggs exploded from the back of Commander Ron's
tights. Charlie doubled over gagging.

The commander turned bright red. 'S-sorry
about that, son . . . It's the Moozem. I f-feel like
I've swallowed a million whoopee cushions.'

'It's okay, Commander Ron,' Charlie said,
pinching his nose. 'It's not your fault.'

'S-son, how come you can s-still move? Why
aren't you p-paralysed like the rest of us?'

'I think my superpowers must be a little bit
different to everybody else's. The Moozem doesn't

seem to affect me in quite the same way.'

Charlie let out a loud burp. 'See what I mean?'

He stretched out his hand. 'Commander Ron, take my hand, I'll carry you out of here.'

Commander Ron pushed Charlie's hand away.

'No, no, son, s-save your strength. You're our last hope now. You're the only one who can defeat that madman out there.'

Charlie looked skywards. 'But sir, I can't do it. That killer robot's too big and strong for me.'

Commander Ron gasped for breath. 'Listen, that robot's not designed to fight someone as s-small as you. Use your size to your advantage. Keep low. Run f-fast. Confuse the robot. Find its weakness. Then d-destroy it. Do you understand?'

Charlie nodded.

Commander Ron reached up, trying to grasp Charlie's arm.

'Son . . . you have to believe in yourself. Remember, it's not the s-size of the dog in the fight that matters . . . it's the size of the fight in the dog . . .'

Charlie held Commander Ron's arm tightly. 'I'll

remember, sir . . . thank you so much. Sir, is there anything else I need to know?'

Commander Ron's cheeks turned red with strain.

**PHRRRRRRRRRRAAAAAAPPPPP.**

'Yes, don't ever strike a match in here, son. Good luck.'

Gagging for air, Charlie staggered away.

# 16

# TIRED, TIED UP AND TARGETED

'General Pandemonium, are you there, sir? It's Sergeant Briggs calling from the spaceship.' The general turned on his communicator.

'Yes, Sergeant Briggs, I'm here, what is it?'

'Sir, the Undie-taker-downer is fully charged and ready to fire at earth.'

'Thank you, Sergeant Briggs . . .'

The general looked down at Josh, who was still in the robot's tight grip. 'Now, my big-mouthed little friend, I think it's time we found something to permanently shut that annoying trap of yours. How about a dip in a pool of Guzarian juice filled with man-eating piranhas? I hear they're especially frisky this time of the year.'

Josh thrashed about, trying to free himself.

'Or maybe a few spoonfuls of Tozotope jelly will do the trick? I hear it dissolves your insides faster than you can say "ouch".'

'Leave me alone, freaky-beak,' Josh shouted. 'If you want to prove how tough you are, then why don't you pick on someone your own size?'

The general stood up and shook his fist.

'Oops,' Josh said. 'I stand corrected . . .'

'Listen, ragweed, nobody talks to the world's most powerful supervillain like that! If I hear one more word from you—'

Suddenly the communicator buzzed again.

'Sir, it's Lieutenant Kurse here. I have some great news for you, sir.'

The general groaned and rolled his eyes.

'Lieutenant Kurse, how many times do I have to keep telling you – never interrupt me when I am in the middle of threatening someone. Don't you know it's the height of rudeness?'

'But sir, this time it's *really* good news.'

'What is it, man?'

'Sir, the prime minister has just this moment agreed to meet all of your demands. The gold, the silver, the diamonds, the yellow squishy nuggets, Panuary, the whole deal, sir. Now we don't have to fire the Undie-taker-downer at earth.'

The general cackled loudly. 'Oh yes we do.'

'I beg your pardon, sir?'

'Lieutenant Kurse, I planned to fire the Undie-taker-downer whether the prime minister met my demands or not. You see, why should I just settle for a small portion of the world's resources, when I can have the entire planet under my control instead? After I fire the Undie-taker-downer I'll be the one wearing the trousers. In fact I'll be the only one left wearing trousers, and that will leave me in charge. The rest of the world will be locked away in their homes trying to conceal their spotty bare bottoms. Brilliantly simple, isn't it?'

Lieutenant Kurse was speechless.

'Besides, think of what it will do for my reputation. After the world sees that I have lied to the prime minister and can no longer be trusted, everyone will be twice as scared of me. You simply can't buy publicity as bad as that!'

Josh screwed up his face. 'No! It's not fair. Millions of pairs of innocent pants are going to be destroyed because of your sick, evil, mind.'

General Pandemonium flicked a switch on his firing controls. 'All right, I can fire the Undie-taker-downer from here. Let's do a quick test run before we blow away the earth's pants.'

He looked at Josh.

'Oh, I think I've found a perfect target.'

Josh gripped his shorts and closed his eyes.

'Noooooooooooooo!!!'

## 17

# BOLD, BRAVE AND BOTTOMLESS

**KERASHH.**

The doors of the sports stadium tumbled to the ground. Charlie stomped out, dribbling and burping.

'Well, well, well,' the general cried. 'If it isn't the return of Zero Boy. So what are you going to threaten me with this time? Are you going to squirt me with detergent? Or rub soap in my eyes?'

Charlie clutched his aching belly.

'**BURRRRP.** Put my friend down – *now*!'

The general burst out laughing. 'You really have no idea when to quit, do you? Honestly, this is ridiculous. Whoever gave you the crazy idea that you could challenge a supervillain like me?'

Charlie let out another loud burp. 'A great man once told me, it's not the size of the dog in the night that matters – it's the size of the fog in the dog.'

The general scratched his head. 'All right, have it your way, then.' He grabbed the robot's controls.

'Okay, STINK-R, let's show this little soap stain what thirty tons of metal muscle can do.' The general activated his microphone. 'STINK-R, *attack*!'

The killer robot lunged forward, then dropped to the ground, raised one of its legs and started licking it.

'***Beep-STINK-R-a-cat. Meow . . .***'

'No, no. STINK-R, you're not a cat, you moron. I said *attack*.'

The general banged the robot's head hard.

'***Beep-ouch-STINK-R-attack***.'

**WHIRR**, **CLANG**.

The robot's claw opened, revealing fifty rocket launchers in its fingertips. **SCHZOOM SCHZOOM SCHZOOM**. Rockets flew at Charlie from every direction.

Charlie put up his hands, smothering the thunderous explosions with his palms. 'Oww! That really stings,' he cried, blowing on his fingers.

'Charlie – look out,' Josh bellowed as a flame thrower emerged from the killer robot's mouth.

In a flash, Charlie dropped to his knees, curled himself over and began rolling forward like an out-of-control bowling ball. He circled round the robot, then weaved in and out between its gigantic legs. **KA-SLAM.** The robot kicked out its feet, trying to squash him.

**WOOSH**. Charlie increased his speed, circling faster and faster. The robot swung its free claw wildly but missed Charlie every time.

'Get him, get him,' General Pandemonium boomed. The robot swivelled about, frantically chasing after Charlie, but smoke started pouring out of its engines.

'No, no, no.' The general pounded the robot's controls.

Suddenly the killer robot overheated and – **KA-CLUNK** – completely seized up.

'*Beep-STINK-R-stuck-stuck-stuck-stuck-*

**stuck . . .**' The snake-like arm dropped down, releasing Josh from its grip.

Charlie jumped up to his feet. 'Okay, General, this is your last chance. I'm warning you, give yourself up – or else!'

'Or else what? You'll get your mummy on to me?'

Charlie raised his fists. 'All right, you asked for it, it's time to take you down.'

The general howled with laughter. 'You – take *me* down? I don't think so, sonny.' He quickly adjusted the Undie-taker-downer's firing controls. 'But I do know of something else that's about to be taken down—'

'What?'

**KA-ZONG.** A brilliant ray of orange light flashed down from space and blasted Charlie.

**KER-FLOP.** His shorts and pants instantly fell to the ground.

'Oh no,' he cried.

Josh covered his eyes. 'I'll tell you something, mate: now would be a great time to be invisible.'

## 18

# USE THE SHORTS!

Charlie desperately ripped off his cape and wrapped it round his waist like a towel.

The general flipped back a glass cover, revealing a large pulsing red button marked **DOOM SWITCH** on the Undie-taker-downer's firing controls. 'Hah, you pathetic pipsqueaks have failed in your mission to stop me. You're too late, the bottoms of the world are about to be bared.'

He grabbed his communicator. 'Lieutenant Kurse – inform the crew of the spaceship that I'm about to fire the Undie-taker-downer at earth.'

The grinning general hovered his finger over the red button. 'This is going to be one small click for a man . . . and one giant *pants-down* for all of mankind.'

'Wait, you big loony!' Josh cried. 'Aren't you

forgetting something? If you push
that button, your pants will get
zapped as well.'

The general glared at Josh.
'Honestly – do I really look
that stupid to you? Listen, butter
brain, I didn't graduate from
the Intergalactic Academy of
Mayhem with an honorary
degree in world domination

for nothing, you know. Of course I won't get
zapped. Duh . . . I've already programmed the
Undie-taker-downer to make sure that it blasts
everything on the planet except for me and the
crew of my spaceship.'

The general leaned forward and tapped his
forehead. 'Brains, sonny, you've gotta have lots of
brains to be an evil genius like me. You can't afford
to miss a single thing.' The general smiled and
pressed the button down hard.

*Warning: password required. Warning:
password required. You must enter a
password to activate DOOM mode.*

109

'What?' He slapped the firing controls. 'This is nuts. Why should I need a password? I'm in charge of the whole blooming operation, for goodness' sake.' He shouted into his communicator.

'Lieutenant Kurse, I've forgotten my secret password; locate it immediately!'

'Yes, sir. Um, is it in your super-secure secret vault, sir?'

'No, Lieutenant . . . I think I wrote it down on a sticky note behind my desk calendar.'

'Roger, sir . . .'

Josh was waving at Charlie like a madman. 'Now's your chance – do something.'

Charlie gripped his cape. 'But I can't move in this thing.'

Josh pointed frantically at the ground in front of Charlie's feet.

'*Use the shorts!*'

'What?'

'Use your shorts – like a sling. Fire a rock or something at the general.'

Charlie quickly looked around but all he could see was grass. He bent over and pulled off one of his shoes. He dropped it into his shorts and started swinging it powerfully above his head.

'Make sure you don't miss – you're only going to get one chance!'

Charlie focused carefully with his super vision then – **HUUMPHHH** – heaved the shoe out of his shorts. The shoe rocketed through the air towards the general but flew over his head and disappeared up into the clouds above.

'Oh no.' Josh held his head in his hands.

Lieutenant Kurse's voice came racing back over the communicator.

'I found it, sir. Your password is miffy-squiffy-sniffy.'

The general entered his password.

**Password accepted. DOOM mode activated. Global destruction authorised.**

'All right, let's do it . . . let's make history.' General Pandemonium placed his finger on the big red button again. But just as he was about to push it down, Charlie's shoe suddenly boomeranged back down from the sky and – **THOCK** – smashed into the general's enormous hooter.

'Arghh!! My nose!' The general toppled over and slammed face first onto the firing controls.

**FZZZARGH**. The controls exploded in a flash of sparks. The large red button started pulsing uncontrollably.

*Warning: Undie-taker-downer malfunctioning. Previous instructions have been reversed . . . Warning: Undie-taker-downer malfunctioning. Previous instructions have been reversed . . .*

The dazed general sat back up in his seat. 'Oh no, what have I done?'

He stood up and furiously tried to stop the Undie-taker-downer from firing.

**Undie-taker-downer about to fire** . . . **Five** . . . **Four** . . . **Three** . . . **Two** . . . **One** . . .

The general looked up. **KA-ZONG**. He was blasted by a brilliant orange light from space.

**KER-FLOP**. His trousers and pants fell down around his knees.

'Arghh!!!' The general turned bright red with embarrassment and tried to cover himself. 'Lieutenant Kurse,' he shouted into the communicator, 'get me out of here this instant – I've lost my pants!'

A sobbing Lieutenant Kurse whispered back. 'I'm sorry, sir, I can't help you – we've all lost our pants as well. The whole crew.'

The general shook his fist angrily at Josh and Charlie. He grabbed his fallen pants and trousers and climbed down the emergency escape ladder.

'You dirtbags are going to pay for this. I'm going to find myself a towel and come back and crush you like cupcakes.'

The general raced off, trying to cover his backside with his billowing boxers.

'That guy has some serious anger-management issues,' Josh observed.

'I know,' Charlie said. 'But I find it really hard to take anyone seriously when they wear boxer shorts with little poodles printed on them.'

Josh turned to Charlie. 'Okay, let's rescue those superheroes.'

Suddenly – **KA-BOOM** – the ground shook like an earthquake. The giant killer robot roared back into life. Charlie froze as a bright red laser beam lit up his body.

'*Beep-stuck-stuck-unstuck-STINK-R-attack . . .*'

Without stopping to think, Josh scrambled up the robot's escape ladder and hopped into the general's seat.

'STINK-R *stop!*' he bellowed. The robot ground to a halt. 'STINK-R, hunt the general and catch him!'

'***Beep-affirmitive-STINK-R-bump-the-general-and-smash-him.***'

Josh jumped back down to the ground and watched the metal monstrosity storm away.

'Thanks, Josh – I owe you one,' Charlie said.

'No problem,' Josh said, smiling. 'Hey, I wonder what the STINK-R will do to the general when he finds him?'

'I'm not sure,' Charlie said. 'But I sure hope, for the general's sake, that he hasn't been programmed to give killer wedgies.'

# 19

# FROM ZERO TO HERO

**Dah-da-dah-da-dah-da-dah-dah!**

Trumpets sounded and the Super School
orchestra struck up to play. Charlie waved to
the crowd as he mounted the dais of the Heroes
Podium. High above, a squadron of junior cadets
flew past in a victory formation. The director of
the Super School, Alfred Heath, stepped up to the
microphone.

'Ladies, gentlemen and students, I'm proud
to introduce the world's bravest new superhero,
Charlie Applejack.'

'**HOORAY!**' A huge roar went up.

'Charlie, I can't thank you enough for what
you have done. You've saved all our students,

116

you've saved all our superheroes, and, most importantly of all, you've saved all our pants.' Mr Heath bent down and picked up a large silver trophy. 'It is my great privilege to present you with the galaxy's highest honour for bravery, the Captain Marvellous Award for Supreme Excellence.'

'HOORAY!' The crowd cheered again. Charlie felt chills race up and down his spine.

'This trophy was first awarded to our founding father Captain Marvellous nearly a hundred years ago, and has been won by some of the most esteemed superheroes of all time. Congratulations, Charlie.'

Charlie lifted the trophy above his head. But suddenly he tripped on the edge of his cape and fell backwards. The priceless award tumbled down the steps and shattered into a million pieces.

'Ooops.' Charlie shrugged his shoulders.

Mr Heath dabbed his forehead with his handkerchief.

'Um, er, Charlie, it also gives me great pleasure

to offer you an invitation to join our world–
famous Super School.'

'HOORAY!' Another giant cheer went up.

Charlie stared into the sea of smiling faces and
spotted Josh giving him the thumbs up. He paused
for a moment, then turned to the director.

'I'm sorry, sir, but I can't accept your offer.'

'Why ever not?' Mr Heath cried.

'Somehow I just don't think I'd fit in here.
Besides, I'm part of a super crime-fighting team
now and I can't let my partner down. I think
we'll do just fine on our own, sir. And, like my dad

always says, sometimes you're better off being a big bowl inside a small fish, rather than being a small bowl inside a big fish, if you know what I mean . . .'

'Um, ah, very well, then.'

Mr Heath shook Charlie's hand. Charlie turned and waved to the crowd.

But as he walked away, a large dark shadow blocked out the sun. Charlie peered over his shoulder. His jaw dropped like a rock.

'C-Commander Ron . . .'

The world's most famous superhero stood to attention and saluted his young admirer.

'Son, I saw what you did the other day and I have just one word to say to you – *Wow*!'

Charlie was lost for words.

'I . . . I . . . Th-thank you, Commander Ron . . . th-thank you so much . . .'

COMING IN SEPTEMBER
2010!

THE
ATTACK OF
THE BRAIN-DEAD
BREAKDANCING
ZOMBIES